P9-BZD-289

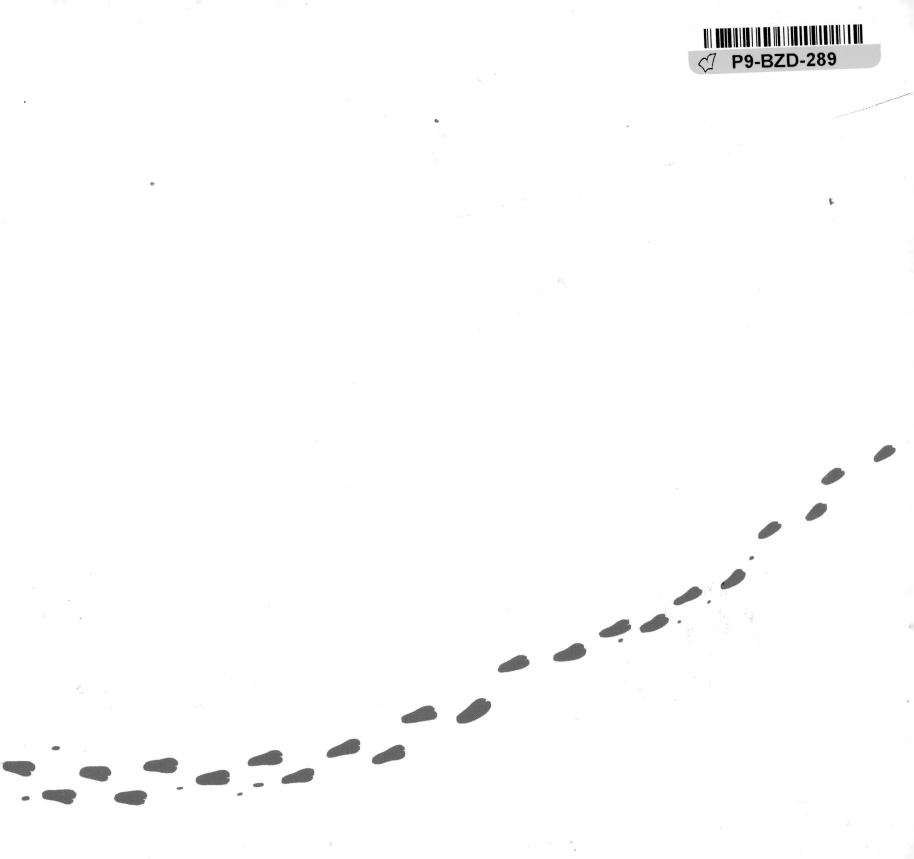

# THERE'S A MOUSE HIDING IN THIS BOOK!

by Benjamin Bird

CAPSTONE YOUNG READERS
capstoneyoungreaders.com

*THERE'S A MOUSE HIDING IN THIS BOOK!*
is published by Capstone Young Readers,
A Capstone Imprint
1710 Roe Crest Drive
North Mankato, Minnesota 56003
www.capstoneyoungreaders.com

Copyright © 2014 Turner Entertainment Co.
Tom and Jerry and all related characters
and elements are trademarks of and © Turner Entertainment Co.
WB SHIELD: ™ & © Warner Bros. Entertainment Inc.
(s15)

CAPS32265

All rights reserved. No part of this publication may be
reproduced in whole or in part, or stored in a retrieval system,
or transmitted in any form or by any means, electronic,
mechanical, photocopying, recording, or otherwise, without
written permission of the publisher.

Cataloging-in-Publication Data is available
on the Library of Congress website.
ISBN: 978-1-62370-125-3 (paper over board)
ISBN: 978-1-4795-5228-3 (library hardcover)
ISBN: 978-1-4795-6160-5 (eBook)

DESIGNED BY:
Russell Griesmer

ILLUSTRATED BY:
Comicup Studio
Carmen Pérez — Pencils
Francesc Figueres Farrès — Inks
Gloria Caballe — Color

Printed in the United States of America in North Mankato, Minnesota.
112017    010964R

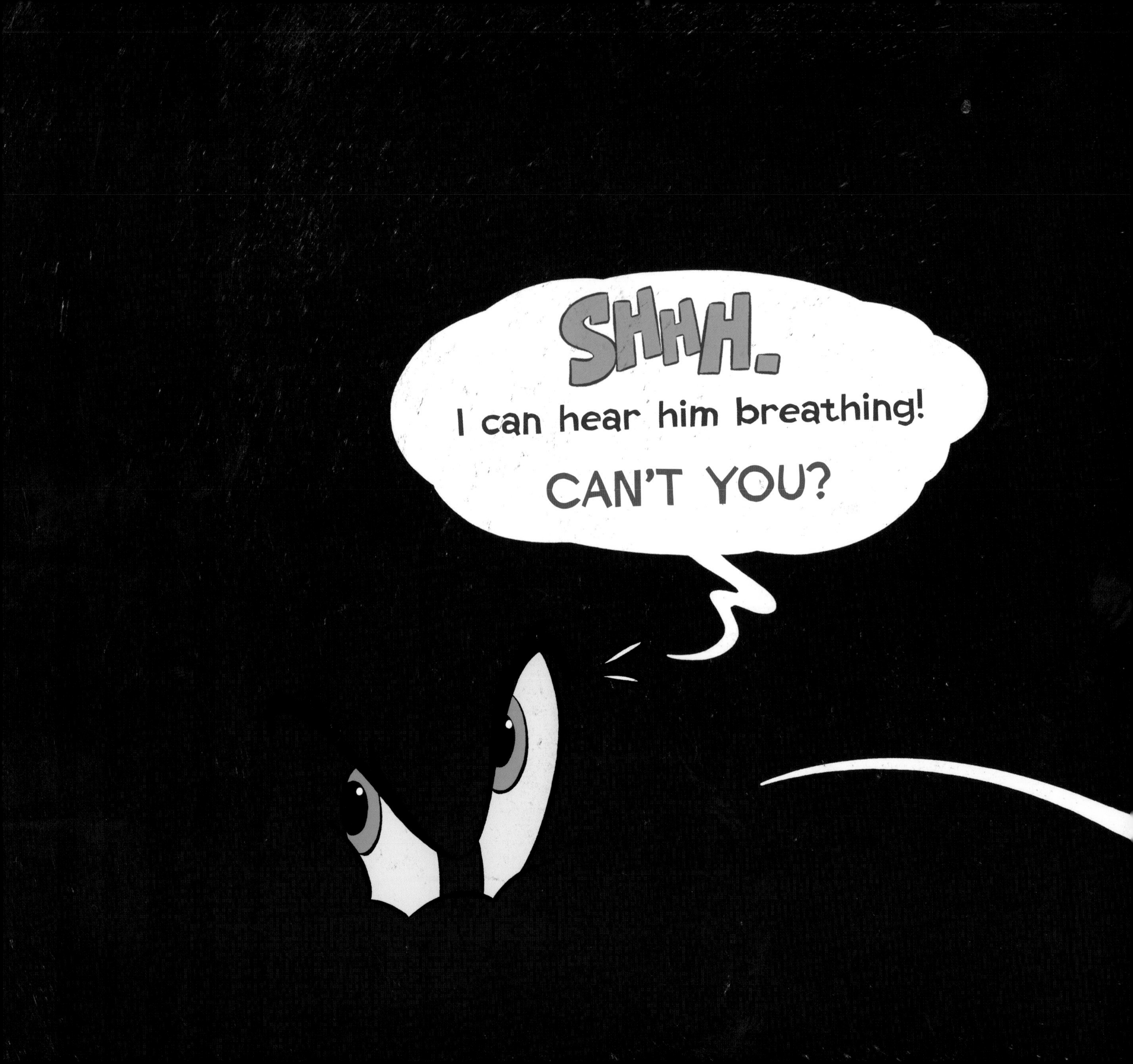
SHHH.
I can hear him breathing!
CAN'T YOU?